THIS WHERE'S WALDO?
BOOK BELONGS TO:

Dania Hernande

Tenango. and Ak

Ael AeL   ALe

First US edition in this format 2012

Library of Congress Cataloging-in-Publication Data is available.
Library of Congress Catalog Card Number 2011047179

ISBN 978-0-7636-5832-8

16 WKT 10 9 8 7

Printed in Shenzhen, Guangdong, China

This book has been typeset in Optima and Wallyfont.
The illustrations were done in watercolor and water-based ink.

visit us at www.candlewick.com

WHERE'S WALDO?
THE SEARCH FOR THE LOST THINGS

A COMPENDIUM OF PUZZLING PUZZLES

MARTIN HANDFORD

CANDLEWICK PRESS

HI THERE, WALDO FANS!

JOIN ME AND MY FRIENDS WOOF, WENDA, WIZARD WHITEBEARD, AND ODLAW ON AN EXTRAORDINARY HUNT FOR OUR LOST THINGS.

WALDO'S KEY   WOOF'S BONE   WENDA'S CAMERA   WIZARD WHITEBEARD'S SCROLL   ODLAW'S BINOCULARS

STRETCH YOUR BRAIN TO ITS LIMITS WITH THE MIND-BOGGLING PUZZLES AND OTHER INCREDIBLE THINGS TO FIND AND DO ALONG THE WAY.

CRAZY CLOWNS, MONSTROUS BEASTS, MUSICAL MAESTROS, MAGICAL MASTERS, AND PLUNDERING PIRATES ARE ALL WAITING TO MEET YOU. AS WELL AS 25 WANDERING WALDO-WATCHERS TO FIND.

INVITE YOUR PALS TO HELP IF YOU LIKE, AND LET THE SEARCH BEGIN!

Waldo

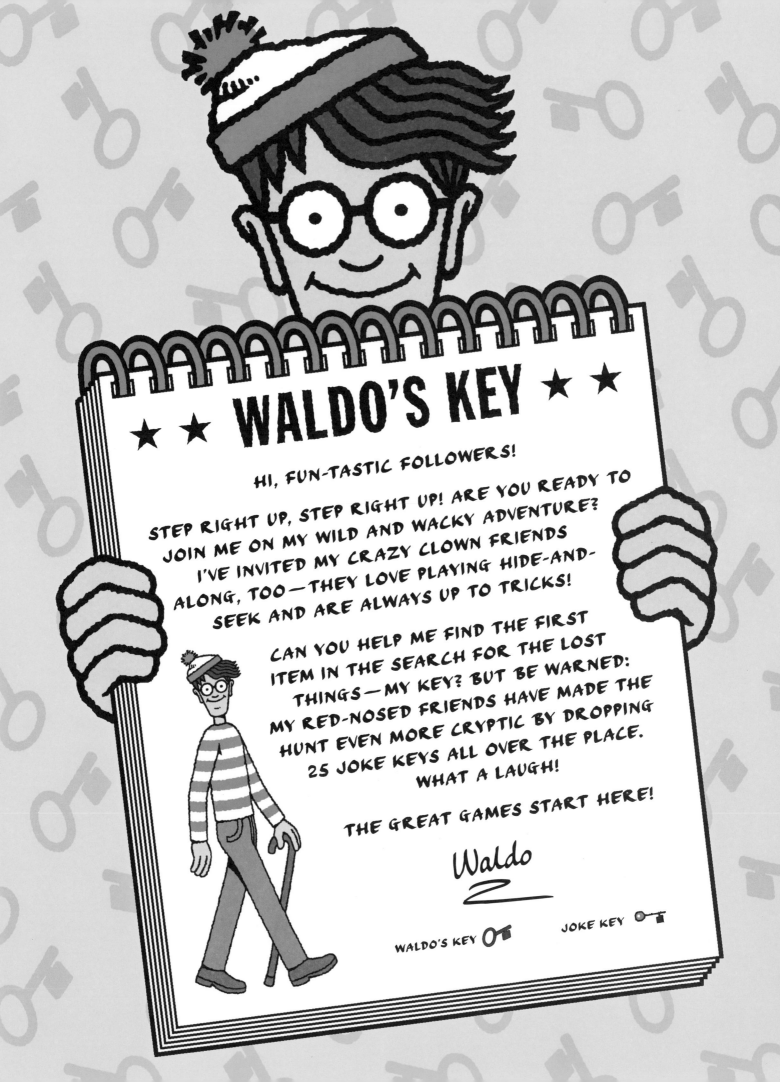

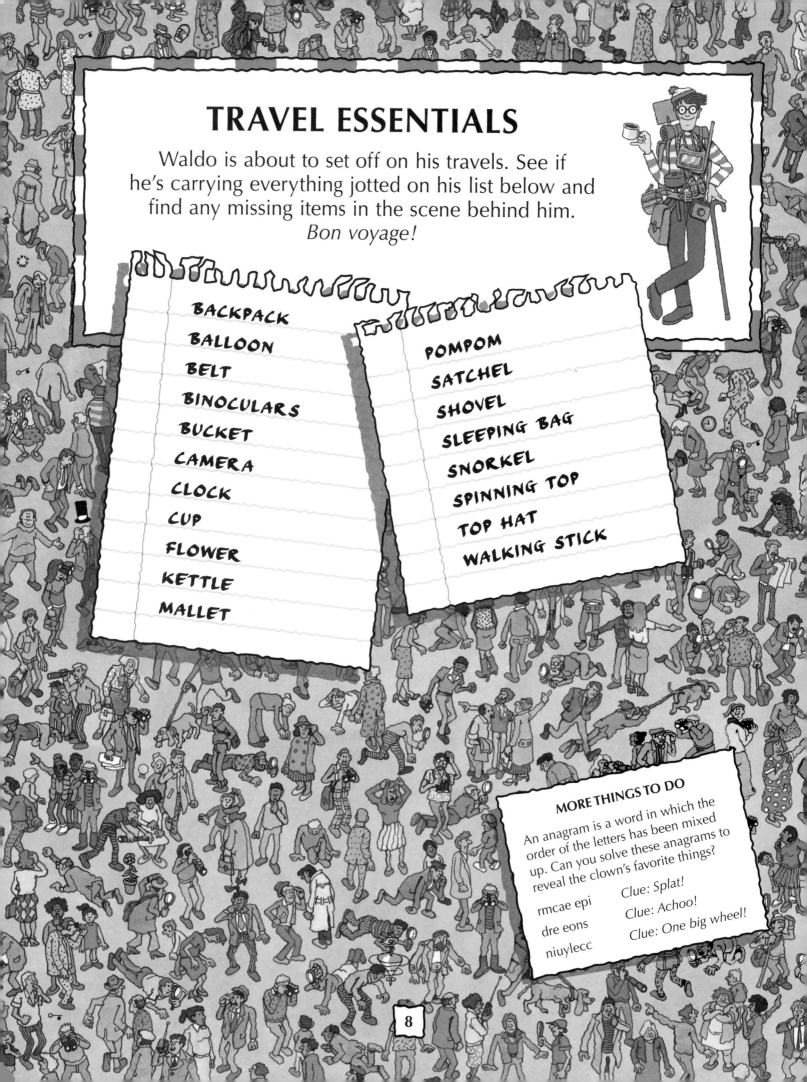

TRAVEL ESSENTIALS

Waldo is about to set off on his travels. See if he's carrying everything jotted on his list below and find any missing items in the scene behind him.
Bon voyage!

BACKPACK
BALLOON
BELT
BINOCULARS
BUCKET
CAMERA
CLOCK
CUP
FLOWER
KETTLE
MALLET

POMPOM
SATCHEL
SHOVEL
SLEEPING BAG
SNORKEL
SPINNING TOP
TOP HAT
WALKING STICK

MORE THINGS TO DO

An anagram is a word in which the order of the letters has been mixed up. Can you solve these anagrams to reveal the clown's favorite things?

rmcae epi   Clue: Splat!

dre eons   Clue: Achoo!

niuylecc   Clue: One big wheel!

DOTTY DOT-TO-DOT

Connect all the *EVEN*-numbered dots in order, and find out
what curiously shaped balloons are floating in the sky.

MORE THINGS TO FIND

☐ Seven cream pies

☐ Eleven blue bow ties

☐ Two clowns wearing the same hat

RED-NOSE RUNAROUND

Connect all the red noses, then all the red pompoms,
and finally all the red balloons to make a maze. Then find
Waldo the *shortest* route to the laughing clowns.

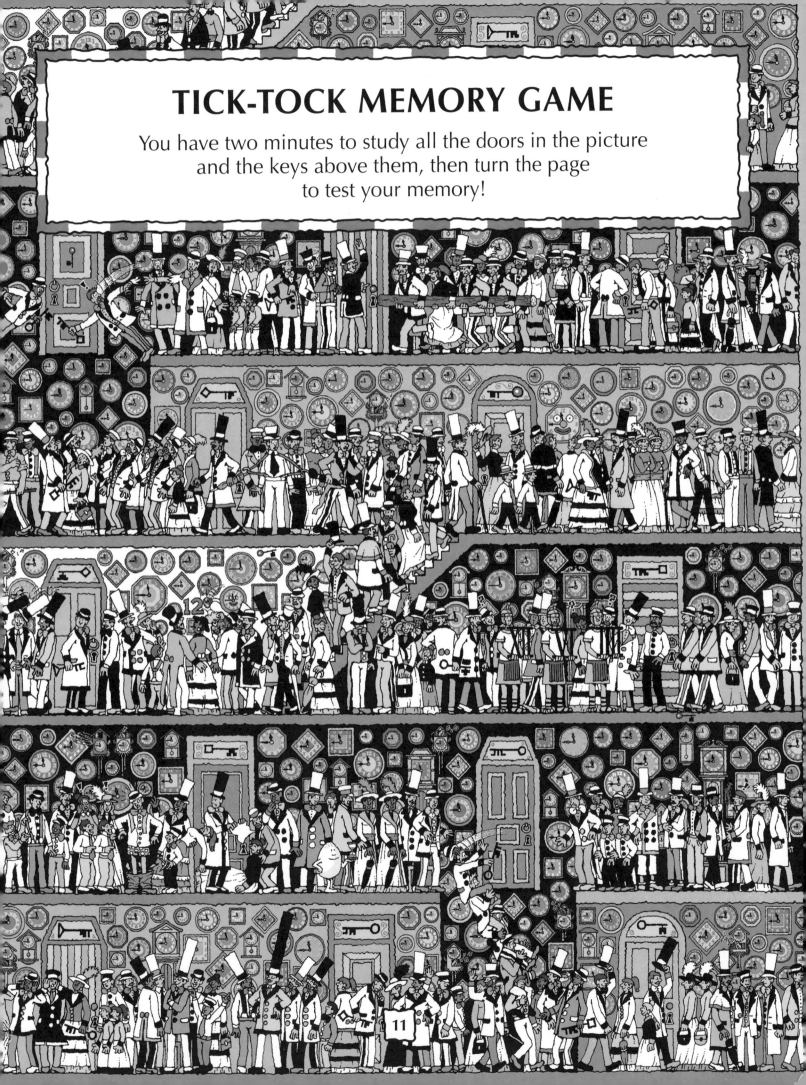

TICK-TOCK MEMORY GAME

Can you remember which key goes above which door
and then draw them in the pictures below?

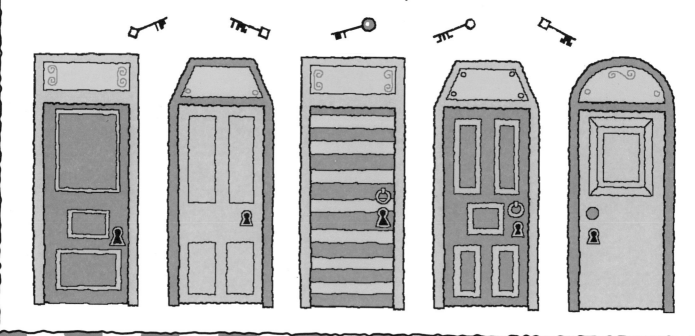

THROUGH THE KEYHOLE GAME

Take your time to peek through these keyholes.
Then turn back the page and find each section in the scene.

HALL OF MIRRORS

In one of these mirrors, Waldo is facing in the opposite direction from the way he's facing in the other three. Can you spot which one?

MORE THINGS TO FIND
- ☐ Four flowers squirting water
- ☐ A punch-in-the-box
- ☐ Someone wearing a chef's hat

PYRAMID PUZZLE

Search for the words at the bottom of this page in the pyramid puzzle.
The words go up, down, forward, and backward.

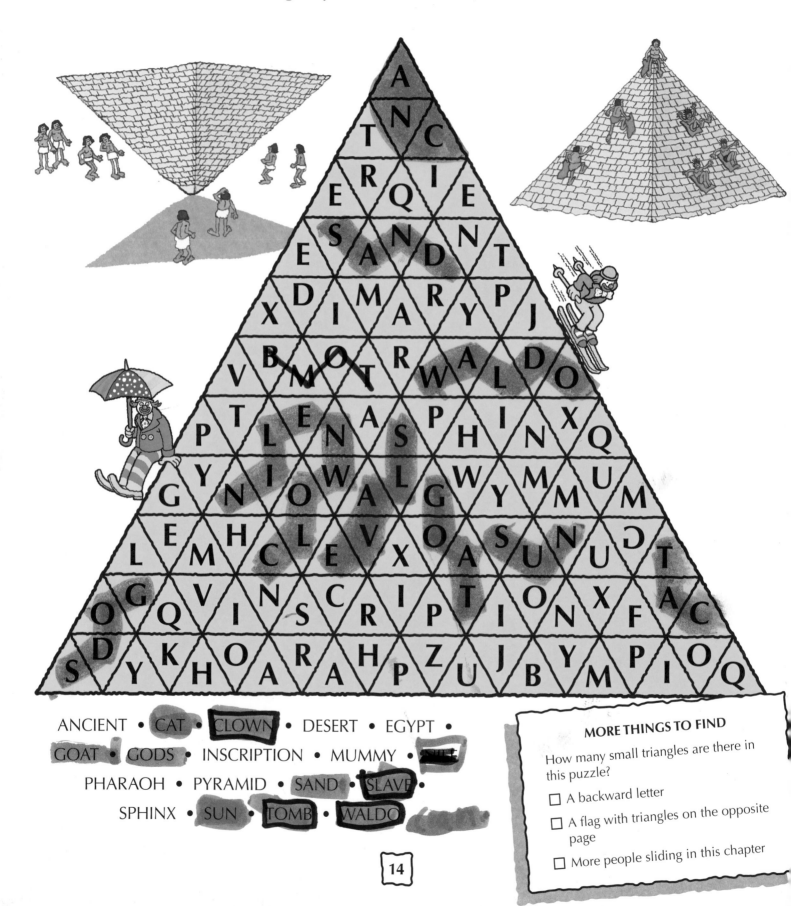

ANCIENT • CAT • CLOWN • DESERT • EGYPT •
GOAT • GODS • INSCRIPTION • MUMMY • NILE •
PHARAOH • PYRAMID • SAND • SLAVE •
SPHINX • SUN • TOMB • WALDO

MORE THINGS TO FIND

How many small triangles are there in this puzzle?

☐ A backward letter

☐ A flag with triangles on the opposite page

☐ More people sliding in this chapter

FUNNY FACE FLAGS

Find these foolish faces in the scene below. Can you also find ten clowns playing hide-and-seek?

MORE THINGS TO FIND

☐ Two snakes

☐ A game of tic-tac-toe

☐ Ten milk bottles

15

GAME, SET, AND MATCH

Clowns love to play games and laugh out loud! Can you copy
these silly faces in the empty squares below them?

MORE THINGS TO FIND

☐ Two exhausted ball players

☐ Five red feathers in headbands

☐ A person wearing a red nose

☐ A man wearing clown shoes

MOON-MAZE MAYHEM

Help Waldo find a path through the moon to reach the red star.

MORE THINGS TO FIND

☐ A horseshoe

☐ Five green aliens

☐ A question mark

☐ An exclamation mark

CRAZY KEY-HUNT GAME

Photocopy the cards on this page as many times as you like and cut along the dotted lines. Then follow the game instructions below and have a friend search for the key!

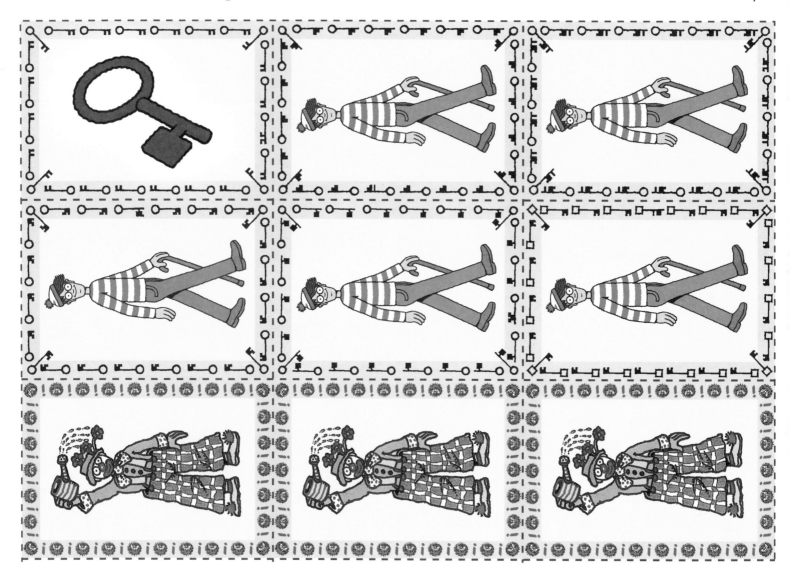

HOW TO PLAY

* First hide the card with the key picture.

* Then write a clue to find the key card on the back of a Waldo card and hide it.

* On another Waldo card, write a clue to where you've hidden the previous one and so on, until all the Waldo cards are used up.

* See how long it takes your friends to find the key! Hide the clown cards nearby. When your friends find one, make up a challenge for them to do before they continue the hunt.

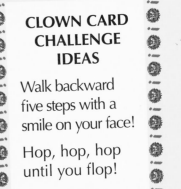

CLOWN CARD CHALLENGE IDEAS

Walk backward five steps with a smile on your face!

Hop, hop, hop until you flop!

Hum a tune!

BALLOON BEDLAM

What a terrific tangle! Follow the strings to find out which balloons Waldo and his friends are holding.

MORE THINGS TO DO

Look at the patterns in the border to find a sequence that matches the order of the patterns on the balloons. Then color in the missing pattern on the empty balloon.

WILD AND WACKY *W'S*

Can you fit all of the *w* words in the puzzle? Then *unlock* the three-letter word that doesn't begin with *w* and find another that has *wandered* backward.

WAHOO

WAVE

WHOOPEE

WHOOSH

WILD

WONDER

WHIZZ

K_ _

WITTY

WOW

WISE

WACKY

REDNAW

SILLY STAMP SNAP

Match each postmark to its stamp by drawing a line between the two.
Then draw a design in the blank stamp and write your hometown
inside the empty postmark.

MORE THINGS TO FIND

☐ An upside-down mummy sarcophagus

☐ Six balloons

☐ A ticklish man

CLOWNING AROUND

Yikes! The clowns have mixed up this picture. Guess who it is and put it in the correct order by writing the numbers 1–6 in the box beside each strip.

WALDO

MORE THINGS TO DO

Find a famous face in a magazine that is large enough to cut into thick horizontal strips. Then mix it up for your friends to solve the puzzle.

SWOOPY, LOOPY RIDES

Doodle a fairground ride on the front of this postcard,
and write a note to your family or friend on the back.

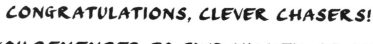

CONGRATULATIONS, CLEVER CHASERS!

DID YOU REMEMBER TO FIND MY KEY, OR DID YOU JUST FIND THE JOKE KEYS? HERE'S A CLUE IF YOU NEED SOME HELP: FIND A SLINGSHOT AND A CREAM PIE . . . AND A VERY NAUGHTY CLOWN WEARING A GREEN BOW TIE.

GOOD LUCK!

Waldo

WALDO'S KEY CHECKLIST

Wait, there's more! Look back over Waldo's journey and find . . .

☐ Three pyramid sand castles

☐ A clown with a cone-shaped head

☐ Three people talking on walkie-talkies

☐ A clown hanging on the end of a fishing rod

☐ Five sets of twin children

☐ A sausage on a fork

☐ A clown with a long blue nose

☐ A woman wearing a white polka-dotted dress

☐ A clock whose cuckoo is escaping

☐ Two clocks with clown faces

☐ A brown bear

☐ A haunted house

Spot one different key in each of the borders of the Waldo Crazy Key-Hunt cards on page 18.

Which page has the most red noses on it? Don't forget to count the ones on the clowns' faces, but don't include those on the *Red-Nose Runaround* maze or the joke keys.

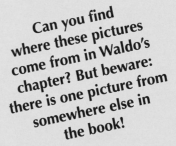

Can you find where these pictures come from in Waldo's chapter? But beware: there is one picture from somewhere else in the book!

ONE LAST THING . . .

Four sneaky clowns have wandered into the other chapters, so keep your eyes peeled and see if you can spot them.

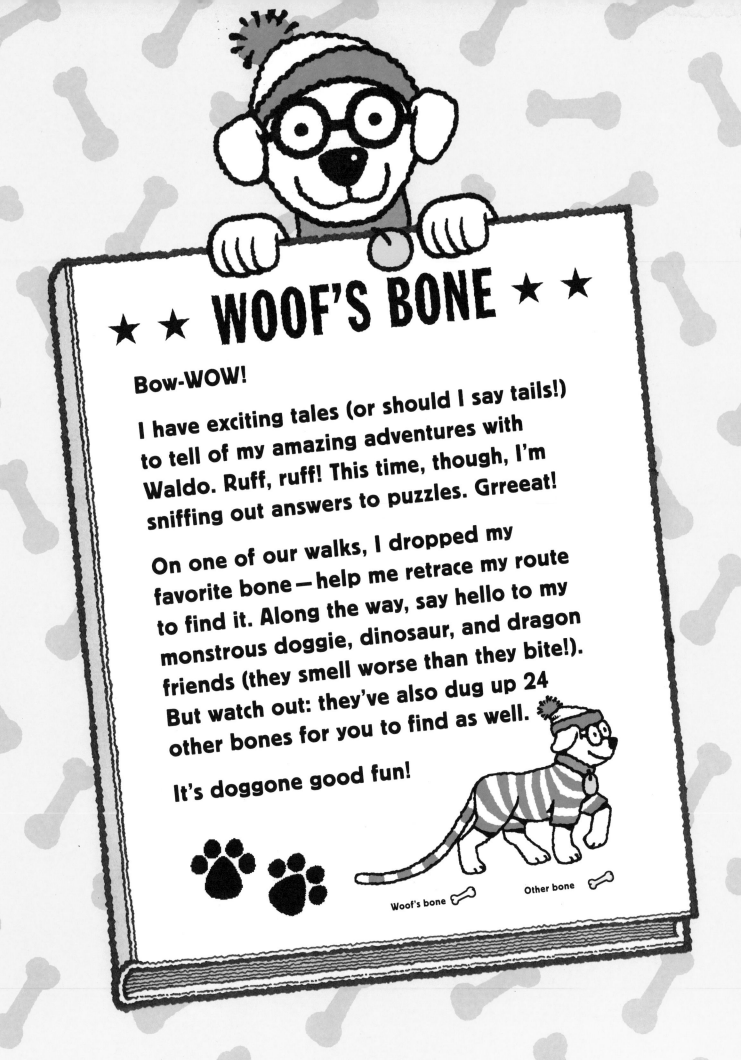

★★ WOOF'S BONE ★★

Bow-WOW!

I have exciting tales (or should I say tails!) to tell of my amazing adventures with Waldo. Ruff, ruff! This time, though, I'm sniffing out answers to puzzles. Grreeat!

On one of our walks, I dropped my favorite bone—help me retrace my route to find it. Along the way, say hello to my monstrous doggie, dinosaur, and dragon friends (they smell worse than they bite!). But watch out: they've also dug up 24 other bones for you to find as well.

It's doggone good fun!

Woof's bone   Other bone

TO THE TAIL END

Find a way through the maze of Woof tails by following only tails with five red stripes. Start at the square with the red tail and use the key below to help you reach the square with the white tail.

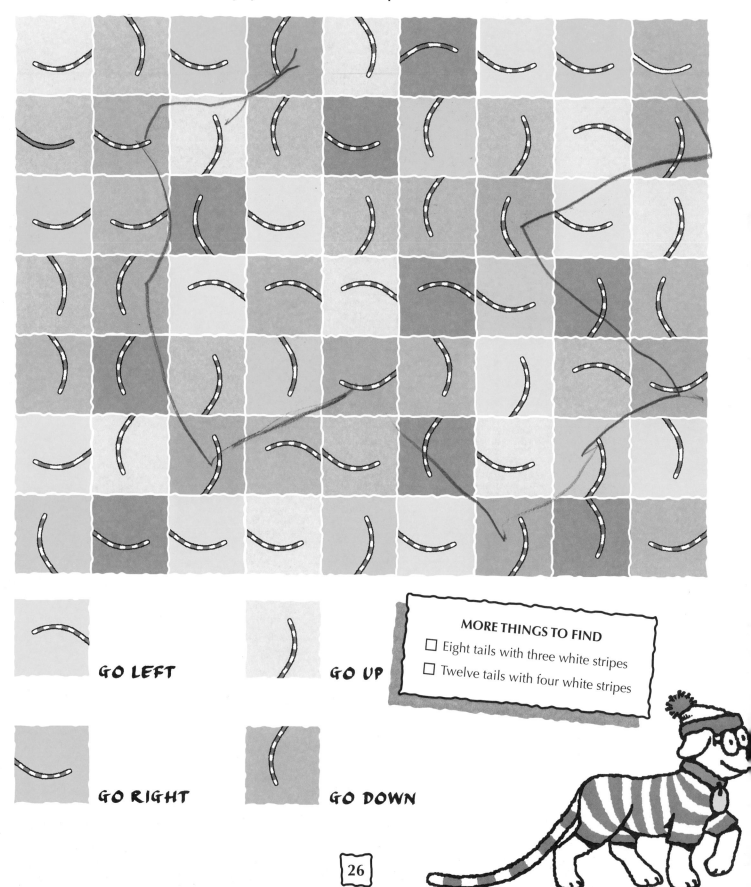

GO LEFT

GO UP

GO RIGHT

GO DOWN

MORE THINGS TO FIND
☐ Eight tails with three white stripes
☐ Twelve tails with four white stripes

MONSTER MADNESS

Can you draw an enormous dog monster in the middle of this scene? Make it as friendly or as terrifying as you like!

MORE THINGS TO DO

* Draw a crest on the white shield.
* Find twelve red-handled swords.
* Color in the white plume.
* Spot a dinosaur!

WHO'S WHO?

What a mix-up! Unscramble the anagrams and fill in the answers in the boxes next to them. Then draw a line to match the pictures to your answers.

OWOF	
GIMNCIAA	
OADWL	
ALODW AWCTERH	
VEMCANA	
IPARET	
RIOSNDAU	
CTAROAB	
IGHNKT	
GIKINV	

MORE THINGS TO DO

Write an anagram of your name in the empty box in the left-hand column. Then test your friends!

BRAIN BONES BUSTER

Take your time to study this scene very closely.
Then turn over the page to test your memory.

BRAIN BONES BUSTER

Here goes! How many of these questions can you answer from memory? (It's also fun to guess!) Then turn back the page to see how you did.

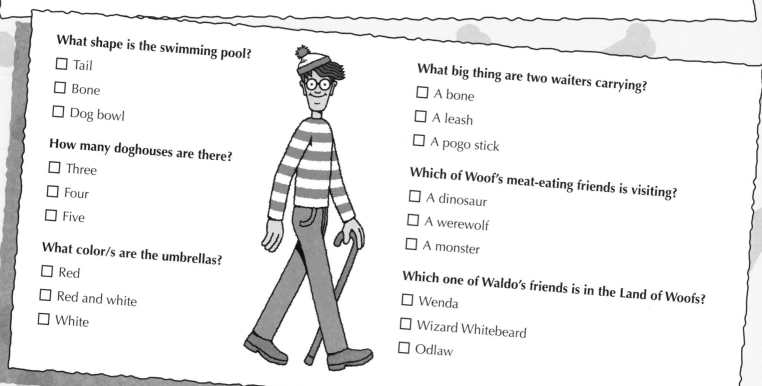

What shape is the swimming pool?
- ☐ Tail
- ☐ Bone
- ☐ Dog bowl

How many doghouses are there?
- ☐ Three
- ☐ Four
- ☐ Five

What color/s are the umbrellas?
- ☐ Red
- ☐ Red and white
- ☐ White

What big thing are two waiters carrying?
- ☐ A bone
- ☐ A leash
- ☐ A pogo stick

Which of Woof's meat-eating friends is visiting?
- ☐ A dinosaur
- ☐ A werewolf
- ☐ A monster

Which one of Waldo's friends is in the Land of Woofs?
- ☐ Wenda
- ☐ Wizard Whitebeard
- ☐ Odlaw

EXTRA BONE-OCULAR EYE-BOGGLER

Study these close-ups carefully and turn back the page to find them.

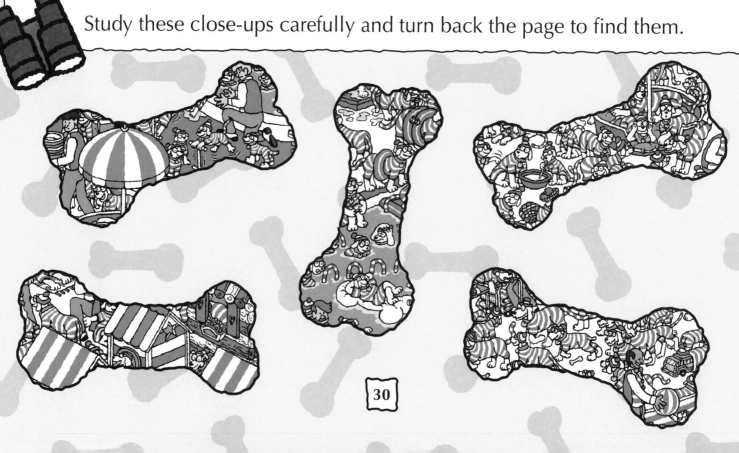

CONNECT THE BONES

Can you connect all nine bones by using only four straight
lines? You may not lift your pencil off the page,
but your lines may go outside the grid.

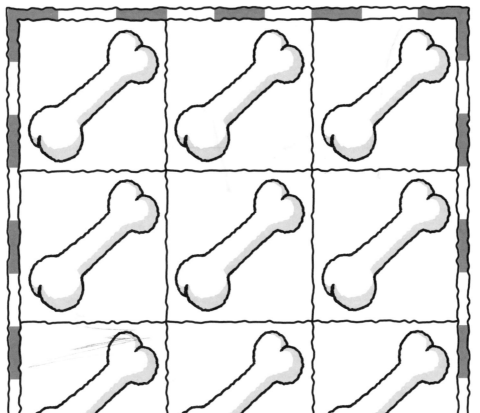

MORE THINGS TO DO

* Join the bones by four lines, taking your pencil off the paper once.

* How many squares are there in the grid? Don't forget that the outer box is a square and four grid boxes also make a square!

* Find three of Woof's werewolf friends in the pictures.

FLOWER POWER

Can you fill in the missing numbers? Each colored group of nine squares must contain the numbers 1–9, as must each row that goes up and down or left to right. You may prefer to write in pencil!

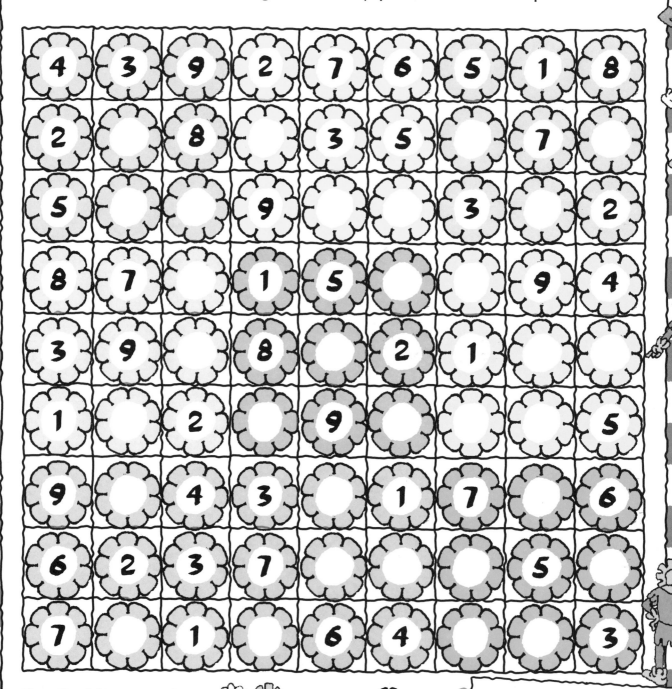

MORE THINGS TO DO

Find these riddles in the picture:

An arrow has sprung a leak.
There's a lot of water—eek!

A man on all fours,
But without Woof-like paws!

BULL'S-EYE!

Help Woof reach the target in the center of the maze by passing all five of his dog pals but avoiding the bulls. It's a-maze-ing!

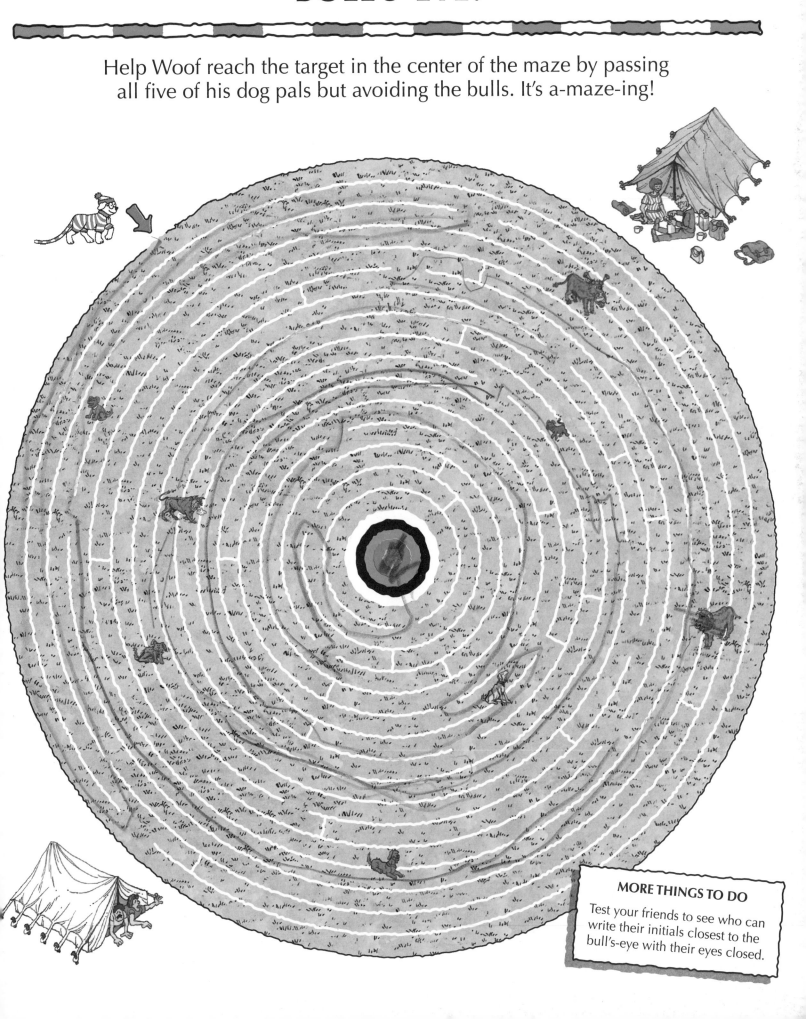

MORE THINGS TO DO

Test your friends to see who can write their initials closest to the bull's-eye with their eyes closed.

WOOF'S WORD WHEEL

Use the clues to help you find five words using three or more letters in the word wheel. Every answer must contain the letter o.

CLUES

It's as hard as rock.

Woof's favorite thing

Used to sniff

Heads, shoulders, knees, and ___

Woof is one of these.

To

Dog

ToD

Sgod

SoD

MORE THINGS TO DO

* Test your friends to see how many other words you can make using the word wheel.
* Look at the scene and find:
☐ A snapped vine
☐ A cave-dog that is a different color from its owner's fur clothes

34

TRUTH OR TAILS?

Test your knowledge of Woof's four-legged ancient friends and work out which statements are true and which are false.

1. Dinosaurs ruled the earth for 160 million years.

2. This is the correct spelling of a type of dinosaur: *parasawralophus*.

3. The brachiosaurus had a very long neck.

4. The ichthyosaurus was a sea creature and is a relative of sharks.

5. The difference between an herbivore and a carnivore was the color of their scales.

6. This anagram spells a dinosaur's name: *uyan toarunsrs xre*.

7. The ankylosaurus had a club tail.

8. A pterodactyl had three wings.

9. Triceratops dinosaurs had a bony frill.

10. There was a dinosaur called diplodocus.

Use the Internet or an encyclopedia to help you—and to look up more fun facts about dinosaurs.

Did you know?

There was an ancient animal similar to a dog! It is called cynognathus (*sy-nog-nay-thus*) and was a hairy mammal-like animal with dog-like teeth. Woof claims that his great-great-great-grandfather was one (calculated in dog years, of course)!

ONE MORE THING!

What is the name of the dinosaur whose skeleton is in this picture? *Clue: It begins with the letter* S.

BURIED BONES

Woof has been busy burying bones! Can you fill in the grid coordinates for the items at the bottom of the page that mark where he has hidden them?

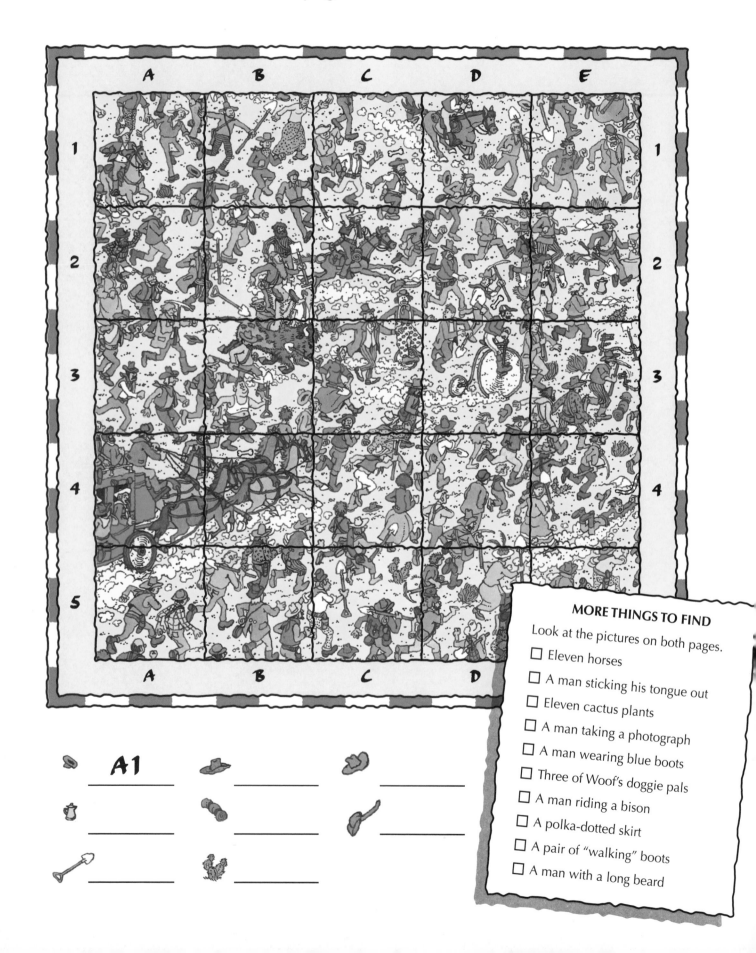

A1

MORE THINGS TO FIND

Look at the pictures on both pages.

☐ Eleven horses

☐ A man sticking his tongue out

☐ Eleven cactus plants

☐ A man taking a photograph

☐ A man wearing blue boots

☐ Three of Woof's doggie pals

☐ A man riding a bison

☐ A polka-dotted skirt

☐ A pair of "walking" boots

☐ A man with a long beard

DIGGING FOR GOLD

Yee-haw! The answers to this crossword puzzle are set in the wild, wild West.

Across

1. A large farm used to keep animals (5 letters)

3. The seat placed on a horse's back (6 letters)

4. A vessel with a handle used to carry water (6 letters)

6. Someone who works with iron and makes horseshoes (10 letters)

9. The opposite of cold (3 letters)

10. A tool used to dig: pick-___ (3 letters)

11. Midday (4 letters)

Down

1. To steal (3 letters)

2. Money offered on a poster for a wanted person (6 letters)

3. A rush of startled animals (8 letters)

5. A green plant with spikes (6 letters)

7. A looped rope used to catch horses (5 letters)

8. A form of transportation on rails (5 letters)

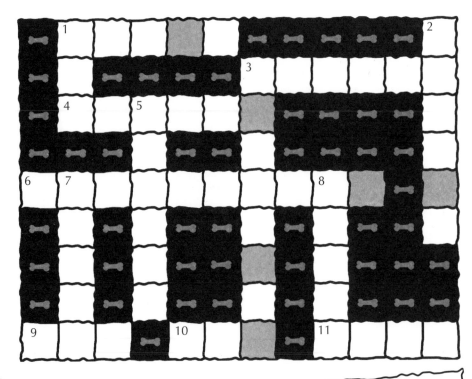

MORE THINGS TO DO

There are six letters in gray squares in the crossword puzzle. Can you unscramble them to spell out grid coordinates and find where Woof has buried some gold coins? The answer will be a letter and a number spelled out in letters.

__ / __ __ __ __ __

NUMBER CRUNCHING

Solve the number puzzle to help Woof jump down through the clouds.
Subtract 1 from any red number and add 1 to any blue number. Then draw a path
to the finish by connecting the clouds that contain a sum of 5.

DOG'S DINNER

To decode Woof's letter, cross out all the *W*'s.
A double *W* means a break between words.

WRWEWAWDWY,WWSWTWEWAWDWY,WWGWO!
WWTWHWEWWRWAWCWEWWIWSWWOWNW!
WWMWYWWCWAWNWIWNWEWWFWRWIWE
WNWDWSWWAWNWDWWIWWWWWAWRWEW
WCWHWAWSWIWNWGWWOWUWRWWFWAWV
WOWRWIWTWEWWFWOWOWDWWGWRWOWU
WPWS—SWAWUWSWAWGWEWS,WWBWOWNWEWS,
WWCWAWTWSWWAWNWDWWEWVWEWNWWM
WAWIWLWMWEWN!

MORE THINGS TO FIND

☐ Thirty-one envelopes

☐ A dog who is not wearing a collar

☐ Two blue dog bowls

☐ A cat dressed as Woof

How many times does the word *wow* appear in Woof's unscrambled letter?

BITES & PIECES

Which three pieces are missing from the jigsaw puzzle? You have five pieces to choose from, so study each one carefully.

MORE THINGS TO FIND

☐ A dog-man holding two bones

☐ A cat on wheels

☐ A man dressed as a poodle

PLAY BALL

Can you work out which rocks come next in these four sequences?
Draw the size of the rocks first, then color them in.

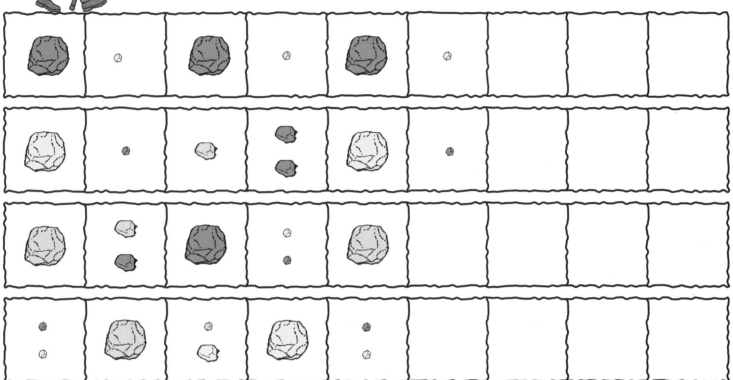

GAME 1

GAME 2

GAME 3

GAME 4

MORE THINGS TO FIND

☐ Ten blue-and-white-striped dinosaurs

☐ A dinosaur with a blue horn

☐ Two red dinosaurs hiding under a pink dinosaur

What a gnashing set of tricky trials, Waldo-watchers— you really are top dogs!

Did you fetch my beloved bone, or were you distracted by all the others? I've retrieved this clue to help you find its whereabouts: sniff out six furry boots and you'll be hot on the tail of my lost bone.

Thanks, cheery champions!

Can you spot these pictures somewhere in Woof's chapter? But hold your horses: one picture is from a different place entirely!

WOOF'S BONE CHECKLIST

Pad back through Woof's wonderful wanderings and find . . .

- ☐ Seven red dog bowls
- ☐ A wanted poster
- ☐ A blue horse
- ☐ A dog-man throwing a stick
- ☐ A rabbit being pulled from a hat
- ☐ Four Woofs with bowls on their heads
- ☐ A man riding a bull backward
- ☐ A red-and-pink-striped dinosaur
- ☐ Three sheep
- ☐ A man sticking his tongue out at a polka-dotted monster
- ☐ Four flying bats
- ☐ Three escaping criminals
- ☐ A hedge in the shape of a watering can
- ☐ A woman wearing a fur coat

ONE LAST THING . . .

Look for many more dogs in the rest of this book. How many can you count along the way?

SNAPPY SINGING!

These stamping feet are creating cracks everywhere in this spectacular singing scene. Can you find eight broken things from the list below?

MORE THINGS TO FIND
- [ ] A smashed mirror
- [ ] Woof's snapped bone
- [ ] A bent umbrella
- [ ] A broken cane
- [ ] A split stage
- [ ] A cracked clapper board
- [ ] A ladder with a broken rung
- [ ] Wenda's broken glasses

MUSICAL FRAME FUN

Wenda has framed her favorite musical photographs. Can you find the picture that doesn't contain a musical note and one with Wenda's face in the frame?

MORE THINGS TO FIND
- ☐ Twelve violins
- ☐ A large bow tie
- ☐ A guitar
- ☐ Three tubas
- ☐ A one-eyed man

CAMERA CLOSE-UPS

Whoops, Wenda's camera is broken! Can you work out who the photo is zoomed in on? Some people appear more than once.

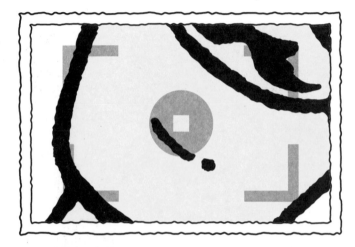

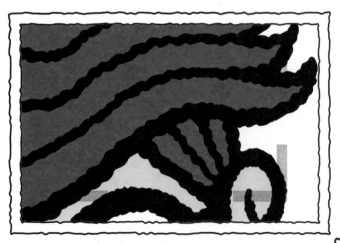

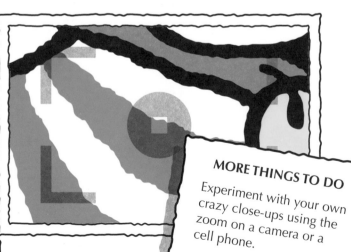

MORE THINGS TO DO
Experiment with your own crazy close-ups using the zoom on a camera or a cell phone.

BUSY BANDSTAND

What a musical muddle! Look at the clapper board and match up the instruments or person with the items needed to play music in a band.

DRUM
CLARINET
CONDUCTOR
TROMBONE
VIOLIN
TRIANGLE
PIANO

MOUTHPIECE
BOW
KEYS
ROD
BATON
REED
STICKS

Rearrange the words below to make the title of Wenda's favorite song. The band is supposed to be rehearsing it!

"A Wonderland Walking in Winter"

MORE THINGS TO DO

✸ Find animal costumes in the scene beginning with *b*, *c*, *p*, and two beginning with *r*.

✸ Sing your favorite song!

A COLORFUL TUNE

Can you find these sets of musical notes in the grid?
The answers run across, down, and diagonally.

MORE THINGS TO FIND
- [ ] A man looking through a porthole
- [ ] A backward note in the puzzle
- [ ] Ten musical T-shirts
- [ ] Five trumpets
- [ ] A man in a drum

LOST LUGGAGE

Spot Wenda and the crew's lost luggage in these photographs.
Wenda's bag has a red-and-white-striped luggage label, and the
crew has nine bags: seven with yellow labels and two with blue ones.

MORE THINGS TO FIND

- ☐ A bag with a red luggage label
- ☐ A man wearing a green tie
- ☐ A woman wearing yellow shoes
- ☐ Woof's tail
- ☐ Two white luggage labels

WOBBLY WORD LADDERS

Hang on! Can you fill in the missing words in these ladders?
Start at the top and work your way down by changing one letter at
a time but keeping the rest of the letters in the same order.

WOW

SONG

DOT

FIND

MORE THINGS TO FIND

☐ A hat with a red pompom

☐ A parrot

☐ Someone sticking out their tongue

Solve the riddle to find the person:

Looking through my hand-held glasses,
I can see closely all that passes.

REELY FUN

Study the tiny pictures in the sprockets of the film reels, and find all the people and things (but not the stars) in the large pictures.

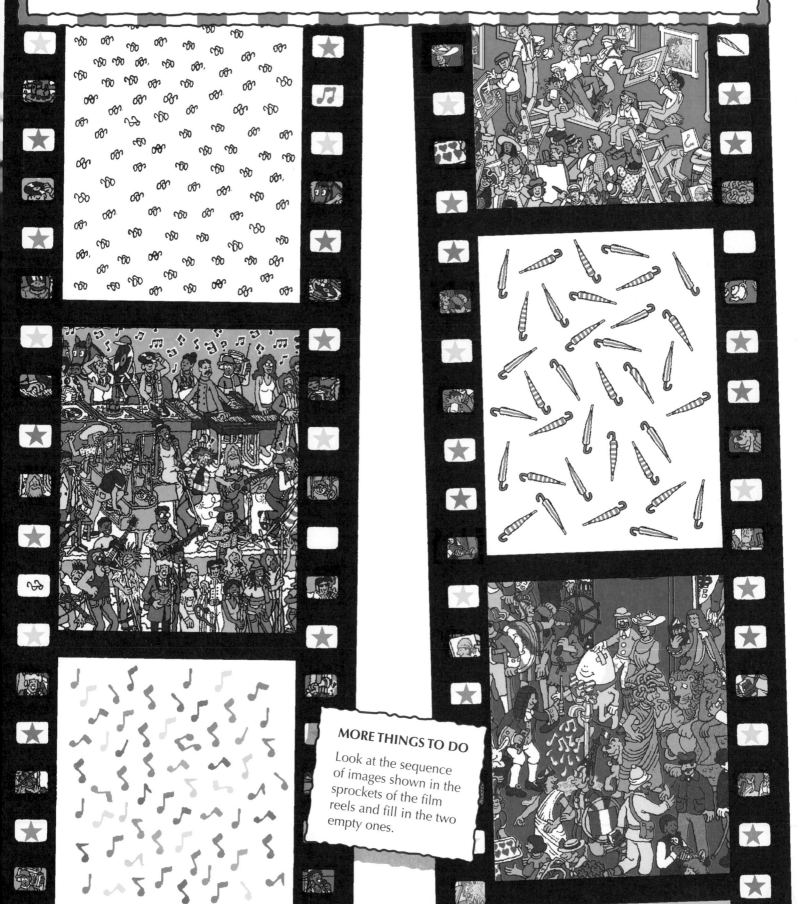

MORE THINGS TO DO

Look at the sequence of images shown in the sprockets of the film reels and fill in the two empty ones.

BEHIND THE SCENES

Oh, no—Wenda's photographs printed out in funny colors!
Only two of these pictures are from the same musical scene—
can you work out which ones?

MORE THINGS TO DO

Write the names of three colors in different colored pens (for example, the word *yellow* in green pen). Then ask a friend to quickly say what colors the words are written in. Do they tend to say the color the words *spell*?

COSTUME COSTS

Wenda has given you $15 to spend. You need to buy one or more of each of the items below, but you may buy only one hat. Remember to subtract the discount from the full price. You must spend all of your money!

Hats $3 ($2 off)   Ties $3 ($1 off)

Shirts $10 ($7 off)   Jackets $10 ($6 off)

$_____
+ $_____
+ $_____
+ $_____
+ $_____
+ $_____
$ = 15

MORE THINGS TO DO

✹ Color in the two black Wenda bills.

✹ Find twelve other Wenda bills in the scene.

BOX BAMBOOZLE

Take a close look at the design on Wenda's unfolded camera box. Which of the three boxes matches the unfolded box? It's a crazily clever combination!

MORE THINGS TO DO

★ How many three-sided combinations does this cube have?

★ Quiz your friends with some of your own cube combinations! Trace the outline of the unfolded box, then draw your own designs on each side.

OH, CRUMBS!

It's snack time backstage! Unscramble all the ingredients for this cake recipe by crossing out the letters in gray that spell *camera* in every word.

CEAGMGESRA

CBAUMTETREAR

CFALMOEURRA

CHOCCAOLAMTEE CRHIPAS

CSAUMGEARRA

CCHAEMRERRIEAS

CCARMEEARMA

MORE THINGS TO FIND

☐ A gingerbread man

☐ Wenda's cake with three red stripes

☐ A double-ended wooden spoon

UNDER THE SPOTLIGHT

Lights, camera, action! Can you spot ten differences between these two musical stage scenes?

MORE THINGS TO DO

Create your own checklist of things to find in the scenes.

☐ ....

☐ ....

☐ ....

☐ ....

☐ ....

☐ ....

WHAT AN EXPRESSION!

Wenda loves catching people unawares in her photographs! Doodle and color in the empty frames and faces to make your own mini portraits.

DANCING SILHOUETTES

Wenda has sent you a postcard from the wrap party. Match the silhouettes with her funky-stepping friends on the dance floor.

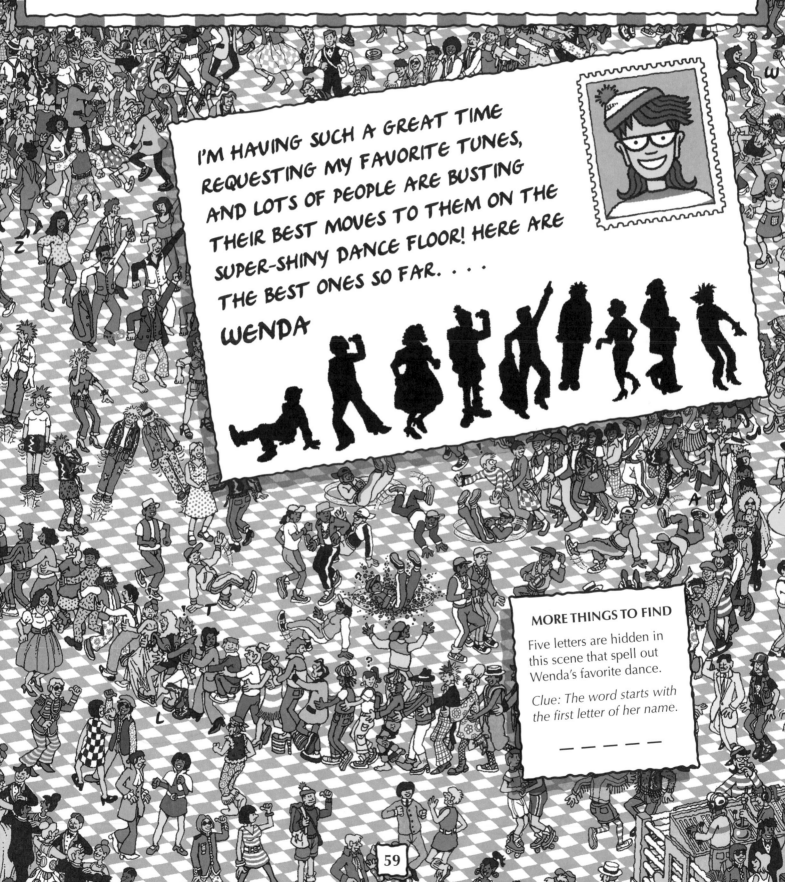

I'M HAVING SUCH A GREAT TIME REQUESTING MY FAVORITE TUNES, AND LOTS OF PEOPLE ARE BUSTING THEIR BEST MOVES TO THEM ON THE SUPER-SHINY DANCE FLOOR! HERE ARE THE BEST ONES SO FAR. . . .

WENDA

MORE THINGS TO FIND

Five letters are hidden in this scene that spell out Wenda's favorite dance.

Clue: The word starts with the first letter of her name.

_ _ _ _ _

WELL, I THINK YOU EARNED YOUR STRIPES AND DIDN'T MAKE TOO MANY "SNAP" DECISIONS. DID YOU FIND MY CAMERA, SEEKERS? HERE'S A CLUE, AND I'M SURE YOUR FRIENDS WILL "LENS" A HAND IF YOU NEED IT: LOOK FOR A TINY HOUSE THAT'S TOO SWEET TO LIVE IN. . . .

BRAVO! ENCORE!

WENDA

Enjoy searching for these pictures in Wenda's chapter. Watch that you don't spend too long looking for one of them, because it's from a different chapter!

WENDA'S CAMERA CHECKLIST
Flick back through Wenda's extravaganza and find . . .

☐ Seven film cans

☐ Two Wendas wearing blue shoes

☐ A frame within a frame

☐ A man with his head stuck in a tap

☐ Frankenstein's monster

☐ Twenty-three ladders

☐ A rabbit man playing the drums with carrots

☐ A couple wearing roller skates

☐ A yellow Woof

☐ A tap dancer

☐ A man painting a nose

☐ Four green striped umbrellas

☐ A man wearing five hats

☐ An Odlaw wearing a red pompom hat

Which page has the most musical notes on it, not including page 48?

ONE LAST THING. . .

Did you spot nine people holding sheets of white paper during Wenda's adventure? These are the crew's lost music sheets, so if you haven't found them, keep looking!

STARS AND STRIPES

Which striped path leads from Wizard Whitebeard's seal to his star?
You better get there quickly, because his spell is making multiple Waldos!

MORE THINGS TO FIND

☐ The end of Wizard Whitebeard's beard

☐ A hat with a yellow pompom

Which striped path crosses the most other paths?

SOMETHING FISHY

Match up the sets of three identically colored fish. One fish is not part of a set, so have a splish-splashing time finding out which one!

MORE THINGS TO FIND

☐ A smiling fish

☐ An angry fish

☐ A fish with closed eyes

SPELL-TACULAR!

These four words have stretched out in a spectacular star shape.
Can you train your eyes to read them?

START HERE!

Clue: Hold the book in front of your nose where it says "start here". Read the word in front of you, then turn the book to the right and read the next word and so on.

MORE THINGS TO FIND

☐ A white suitcase

☐ A striped rocket

☐ A green boot

☐ A frog

GIANT GAME

Start on the board-game square next to each player's picture.
Then follow their footstep guide to figure out who picks up the scroll.

MORE THINGS TO FIND

☐ Nine men wearing helmets

☐ Someone wearing blue-and-yellow tights

☐ Four pitchforks

65

MIX-UP MADNESS

What a muddle! Match the top halves of these characters to the correct bottom halves.

MORE THINGS TO DO

* Draw your own fantasy characters in the two blank boxes! Flip through the book for inspiration for a top half and a bottom half.

* Give some of the mixed-up characters combination names, such as Vikingator (Viking + gladiator).

TWO BY TWO

Wizard Whitebeard is helping Noah get pairs of animals onto his ark. Connect the numbered red dots in order, and reveal a creature that wants to travel on its own.

MORE THINGS TO FIND

☐ An elephant shaped tree

☐ Another Noah's ark in this chapter

☐ A bird's nest

WORD CASTLE

Find the words at the bottom of this page in the three-letter bricks of this castle. A word can read across more than one brick.

R	O	F		A	R	A	M	I	D					A	X	E
M	X	A		J	O	P	W	W	O					W	G	R
L	W	A	D	R	A	W	B	R	I	D	G	E	H	L	D	R	A
F	L	A	G	L	V	N	E	K	R	C	A	T	A	P	U	L	T
N	T	P	C	A	S	T	L	E	L	Q	P	U	F	M	P	X	E
W	Q	T	E	U	F	Y	U	X	H	D	A	B	A	T	T	L	E
M	O	A	T	H	Y	K	W	S	E	J	I	U	L	E	I	A	F
D	G	E	M	I	L	A	I	N	S	I	F	O	R	T	A	F	R
A	R	R	O	W	H	R	E	E	A	K	L	K	C	E	T	L	H
H	F	M	A	R	A	W	N	P	M	T	L	H	F	L	A	G	T
W	A	L	L	T	O	H	Y	O	E	A	B	O	W	P	C	G

MORE THINGS TO FIND

☐ A word that features twice in the puzzle

☐ Two magic words that can open the castle drawbridge

Clue: ten letters that go up, across, and down

O _ _ _ / _ _ S _ _ E

ARROW
AXE
BATTLE
BOW
CASTLE
CATAPULT

DRAWBRIDGE
FLAG
FORT
MOAT
RAM
WALL

68

SHIELDS AND STAVES

En garde—eyes at the ready! Find two pictures that are the same.

MORE THINGS TO FIND

Which color frames are there most of?

☐ Four blue shields

☐ Eight green hats

☐ A carved red staff

☐ A man with stars above his head

GENIE-OUS!

Draw in the missing symbols to release the genie from its lamp!
All nine symbols must appear once in each box,
but never in the same row.

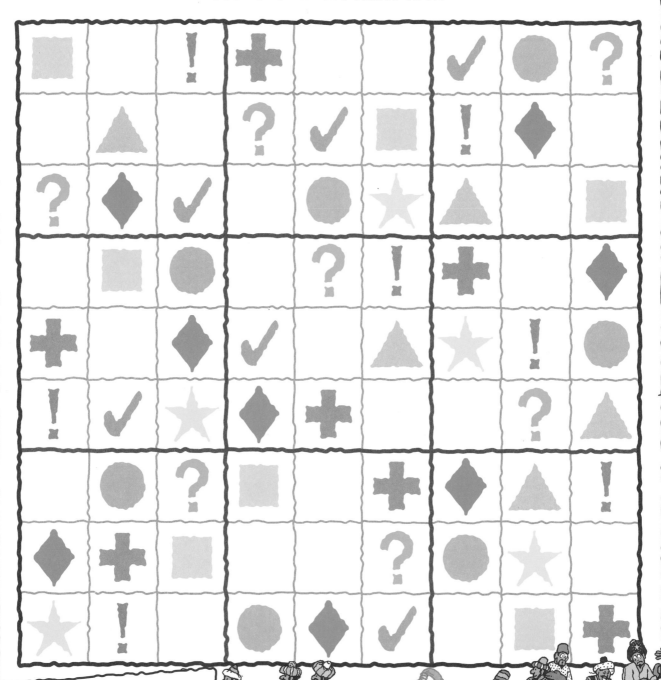

MORE THINGS TO DO

If you were granted three wishes, what would they be?

1. ....

2. ....

3. ....

DOUBLE VISION

All is not what it seems with these magic monks and red-cloaked ghouls. Spot six differences.

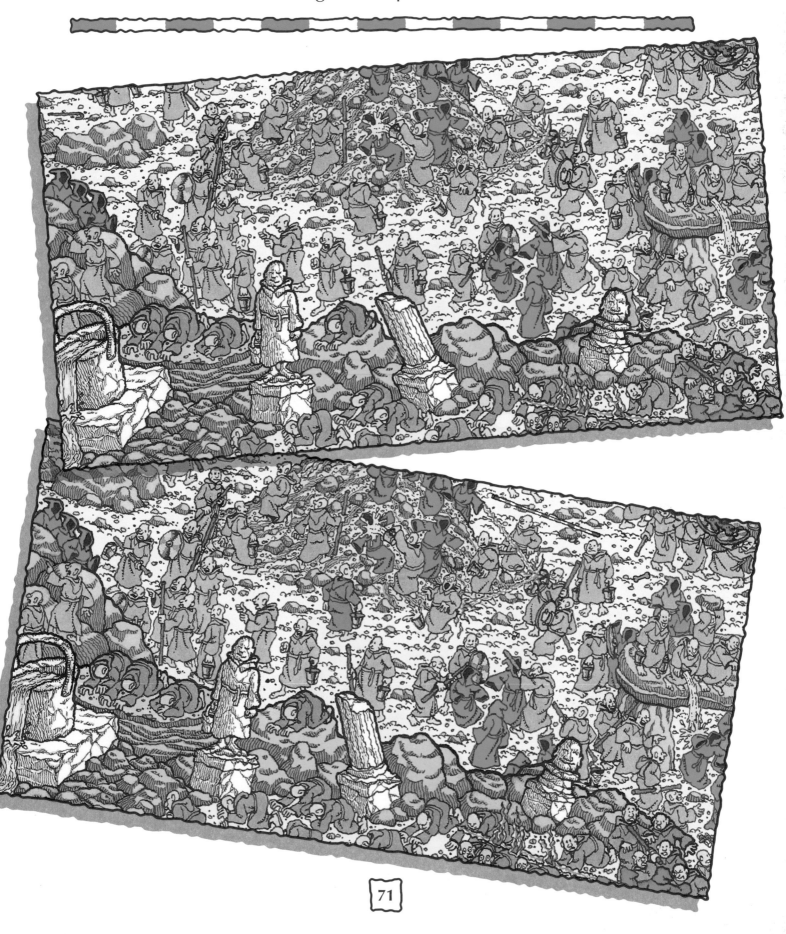

FRUIT PUNCH

Study the fruit in the puzzle closely—to the left and right, above and below. There are two *zesty* kinds of fruit that are always next to each other. Can you fill in the empty squares to keep them paired up?

MORE THINGS TO FIND

☐ Six blueberries in blue berets

☐ A pineapple tickling an apple

☐ Four bananas on sticks

☐ A spoonful of sugar

☐ An apple slipping on a banana skin

DRAGON DELIGHT

A dragon flying competition is about to begin. Draw lots of other dragon contestants to take part in it!

MORE THINGS TO DO

Choose your favorite dragon (it might be one you have drawn) and give it a name. What do you think its eggs look like, and what is its favorite food?

Look at the picture and find:

☐ A dragon with a very long tail

☐ A dragon egg

☐ A red-polka-dotted bag on a stick

HAT TRICK

Wow! Pow! Kazam! Draw tiny people underneath the hats to create your own scene.

MORE THINGS TO DO

✶ Draw in Waldo, Wizard Whitebeard, and Odlaw underneath their hats.

✶ Make your own wizard hat!

WHICH WITCH IS WHICH?

Read the witchy riddles and match them to the pictures.

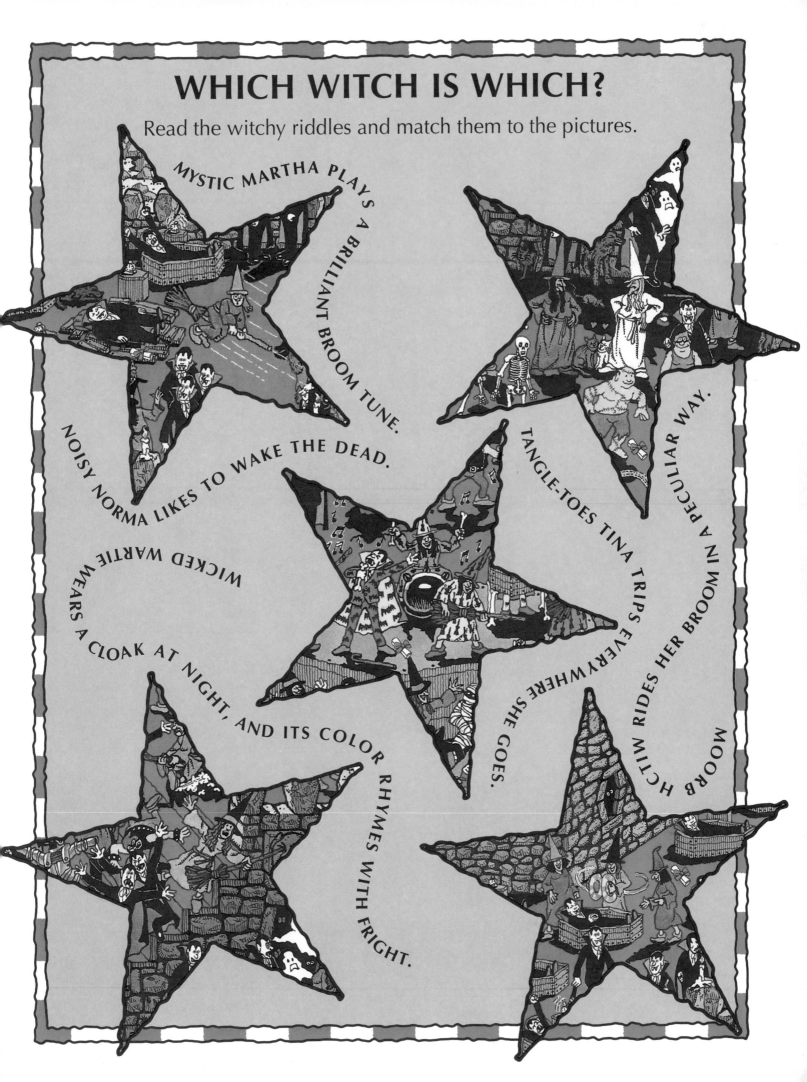

MYSTIC MARTHA PLAYS A BRILLIANT BROOM TUNE.

NOISY NORMA LIKES TO WAKE THE DEAD.

WICKED WARTIE WEARS A CLOAK AT NIGHT, AND ITS COLOR RHYMES WITH FRIGHT.

TANGLE-TOES TINA TRIPS EVERYWHERE SHE GOES.

WITCH MOLLY RIDES HER BROOM IN A PECULIAR WAY.

WISE CRACKS

Wizard Whitebeard has cast a happy spell! This scroll is inscribed with some jokes. Which one makes you laugh the most?

WHAT'S SO SPECIAL ABOUT THE WAY WIZARDS SERVE THEIR TEA?

THEY GIVE IT TO YOU ON A FLYING SORCERER!

HOW MANY WIZARDS DOES IT TAKE TO CAST A SPELL OF INVISIBILITY?

I DON'T KNOW, I CAN'T SEE THEM!

WHAT'S THE BEST WAY TO DESCRIBE A WIZARD'S BOOK?

SPELLBINDING!

WHY CAN'T WIZARDS CLEAN FLOORS?

BECAUSE THE WITCHES STOLE THEIR BROOMS!

WHAT DO YOU CALL A LAUGHING POTION?

MAKES-YOU-GIGGLE-A-LOT-IOUS!

MORE THINGS TO DO
* Make up your own joke in the space on the scroll and test it on your friends.
* Try out five different laughs!

STUPENDOUS SORCERERS! I'M STILL DISCOMBOBULATED ABOUT WHERE MY MAGIC SCROLL IS HIDING. I HOPE I DIDN'T TURN IT INVISIBLE! DID YOU SPOT IT, ALONG WITH THE IMPRESSIVE NUMBER OF BLUE-RIBBONED SCROLLS I CREATED?

I'VE CONJURED UP A RIDDLE CLUE TO FOCUS OUR MINDS: SEEK OUT A MAN WITH A LONG WHITE BEARD AND ABOVE HIM A HANGING SIGN. THE SCROLL IS BUT A WHISKER AWAY!

Whitebeard

A mermaid's tail

Candle wax

Green gloop

Dinosaur spines

Wizard Whitebeard needs an able apprentice to find these special spell ingredients. Look through the book so far and gather them as fast as you can!

A jest of lemon

Egg timer

WIZARD WHITEBEARD'S SCROLL CHECKLIST

Cast your eyes over Wizard Whitebeard's quest and find . . .

- ☐ Wizard Whitebeard in a boat
- ☐ Someone blowing a whistle
- ☐ A man wearing a "bow" tie
- ☐ A snake shaking maracas
- ☐ A flag with five faces
- ☐ A sea lion
- ☐ Nine gold crowns
- ☐ A windmill
- ☐ Someone rolling a die
- ☐ Three wicker baskets
- ☐ Four jumping fish
- ☐ A gargoyle breathing fire
- ☐ A doll in a teacup
- ☐ Three genies
- ☐ A crosswalk
- ☐ A red man who has jumped through a shield
- ☐ A wishing well
- ☐ A skeleton

ONE LAST THING . . .

How many stars can you find in Wizard Whitebeard's chapter (not counting the star bullet points in the *More Things to Do* boxes)?

DISGUISE, DISGUISE!

Beware: here are twelve Odlaws, but, which is the real one? Remember: Odlaw is pictured on the previous page if you need some help!

THINGS TO DO

olor in the
dlaws!

an you spot
omething off
the pattern

SUPER-SNEAKY SEA-GAZING GAME

Odlaw loves to travel the sea with his pirate friends. Study the scene *very* closely and spot the men noted in the ship's logbook below.

☐ Three men wearing skull-and-crossbones T-shirts

☐ Two men wearing hats with green feathers

☐ Three men with yellow beards

☐ Four men wearing red-and-white-striped pants

☐ Three men in yellow bandanas with black dots

☐ Three men holding gold chalices

SUPER-SNEAKY SEA-GAZING GAME

How closely did you study Odlaw's pirate scene? Look through these binocular views and spot them on the previous page.

RIDDLING RIDDLES AND TWISTY TONGUE TWISTERS

How many times can you repeat
**Black and yellow stripes,
Yellow and black stripes**
without getting tongue-tied?

Can you decode this riddle
to find out who is keeping Odlaw
company aboard ship?

*My hands hang low,
But my tail swings high.
See if you can spot me,
Dangling in the sky.*

Repeat this sentence
five times and see how
tangled your tongue gets:
**Pirate plunderers
seek scallywag
scupperers.**

What am I?
*I have eight legs and two big eyes,
but don't look for me in the skies.*

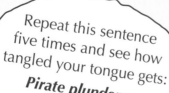

TOP FIENDS

Meet Odlaw's ferocious team of fiends. Look at the pictures
on the cards below and match them to the correct description.

Name: Hungry Growler

Home: Swamps

Favorite Food: Everything and anything

Speed: Lumbering

Courage: 10

Spy Ability: 2

Fear Factor: 8

Special Skill: Roaring and emitting foul smells

Name: Heave-Ho Henry

Home: Dungeons

Favorite Food: Nuts and bolts

Speed: Slow when rusty

Courage: 4

Spy Ability: 9

Fear Factor: 10

Special Skill: Sneaking up on people

Name: Warty Gretel

Home: The Witch's Castle

Favorite Food: Bats' tails, frogs' legs, eyes of a newt

Speed: Fast on a broom

Courage: 4

Spy Ability: 10

Fear Factor: 6

Special Skill: Potions and curses

Name: Captain Cutlass

Home: *The Black Skull*

Favorite Food: Dried meats

Speed: Peg-leg slow

Courage: 9

Spy Ability: 6

Fear Factor: 6

Special Skill: Pillaging

MORE THINGS TO DO

* Who is your favorite fiend on this page?
* Who is the best spy?
* Who is the most courageous?
* Who is the most terrifying?
* Who do you think would own a crystal ball?

SKULDUGGERY

Odlaw has mixed up the skull-and-crossbones flag!
Can you draw it in the right order in the grid below?

MORE THINGS TO FIND
Which one of Odlaw's villainous friends on this page has appeared somewhere else in this book?

Clue: It's a bloodcurdling choice that will chill you to your bones!

SEA MONSTERS

Hear no evil, sea no evil! Color in this monstrous lighthouse scene.
Even the pirates were afraid when their ship sailed past it!

MORE THINGS TO FIND

- [ ] Seven spotted sea dragons
- [ ] Nine ladders
- [ ] A sea dragon flying upside down
- [ ] A pirate in striped clothes
- [ ] A sea dragon wearing flying goggles

SLIPPERY SEARCH

Using your finger, trace a path through the tunnels to help Odlaw escape and pick up his slithery black-and-yellow-striped companion on the way.

86

MAGNIFIED MISCHIEF

Which one of Odlaw's magnifying lenses reveals
striped snakes, birds, and monkeys?

MORE THINGS TO FIND

- [ ] Eleven piranhas
- [ ] Two gold crowns
- [ ] Three broken spears
- [ ] Eleven blue hats
- [ ] A snake staff
- [ ] A black-and-white shield
- [ ] A pirate hat

SNAKING WORDS

Read the clues and work out the answers by connecting the letters inside each frame without taking your pen off the paper!

Clue: A sea-traveling invader

N I
G K
V I

Clue: A sword-swishing soldier

E T E
K M E
S U R

Clue: A skeletal symbol used by pirates

K S S E B S
U A N N O S
L L D C R O

MORE THINGS TO FIND

☐ Ten yellow-headed birds

☐ Three vampires

☐ A flying witch

☐ Frankenstein's monster

☐ A pirate woman

SWASHBUCKLING CHAOS

Can you complete this jigsaw puzzle? Watch out: there's an extra piece!
You could photocopy the page and cut out the pieces if you like.

MORE THINGS TO FIND

- ☐ A scene in one jigsaw piece that is repeated elsewhere in the book
- ☐ Two musketeers with green faces
- ☐ A checkered flag
- ☐ Six musketeers wearing blue tunics with yellow crests
- ☐ A musketeer dog statue

SNAKES AND LADDERS

Waldo and Odlaw are playing snakes and ladders!
Follow the instructions to work out who wins.

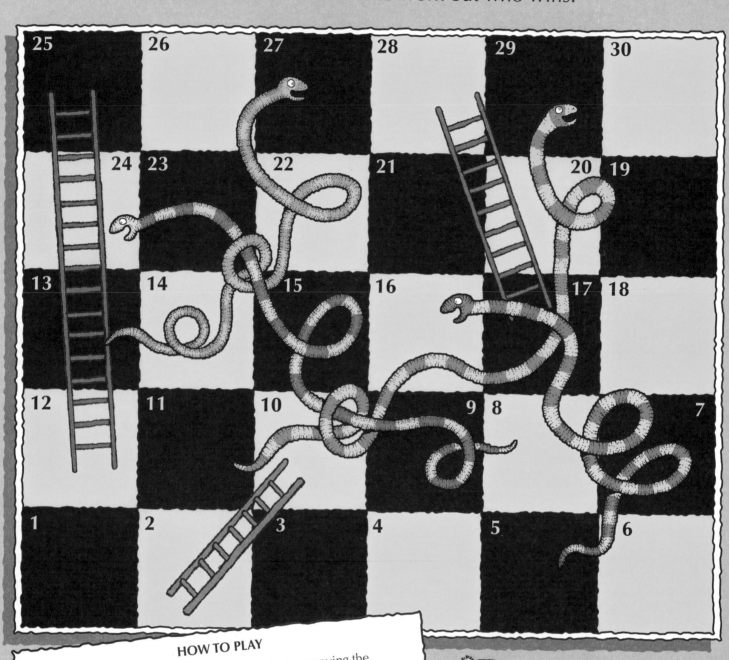

HOW TO PLAY

○ Have Odlaw and Waldo take turns, each time moving the number of squares indicated by their "dice roll" shown at right.

○ So Odlaw goes first, moving two squares, then Waldo goes, moving four squres, and so on.

○ If a player's turn ends on a square at the bottom of a ladder, he should go up it.

○ If a turn ends on a square with a snake's head, the player slides down it.

○ The winner is the player who lands on square number 30 first.

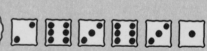

MORE THINGS TO DO
Find a die and play your own game of snakes and ladders with your friends.

FLIP-FLOP SILHOUETTES

Sit opposite a friend, so you both have a scene facing you.
See who can find the silhouettes in their scene first—but beware:
only four silhouettes appear in each scene!

LAND AHOY!

Study the pictures of the extraordinary lands Odlaw has sailed to and fill in the answers to each question below.

How many yellow birds?

_____

How many yellow cream pies have been thrown?

_____

How many pairs of sunglasses?

_____

How many yellow balls?

_____

How many yellow fish?

_____

How many sleeves with black-and-yellow stripes?

_____

MORE THINGS TO DO

Add up all your answers to the questions above and turn to that page number. Can you spot Odlaw's yellow-and-black luggage label?

How many black mustaches?

_____

PIRATEY PUZZLE

Ahoy there! Fill in the answers next to these questions to reveal a word going downward that is Odlaw's favorite piece of piratey disguise!

The _____ seas (*clue: number of days in a week*)

Observing in secret

The rear part of a ship

Person in charge of the ship and its crew

Odlaw's treasure-hunting shipmates

Message in a _____

A heavy weight on a rope that keeps a ship in one place

Pieces of _____ (*clue: a number between 7 and 9*)

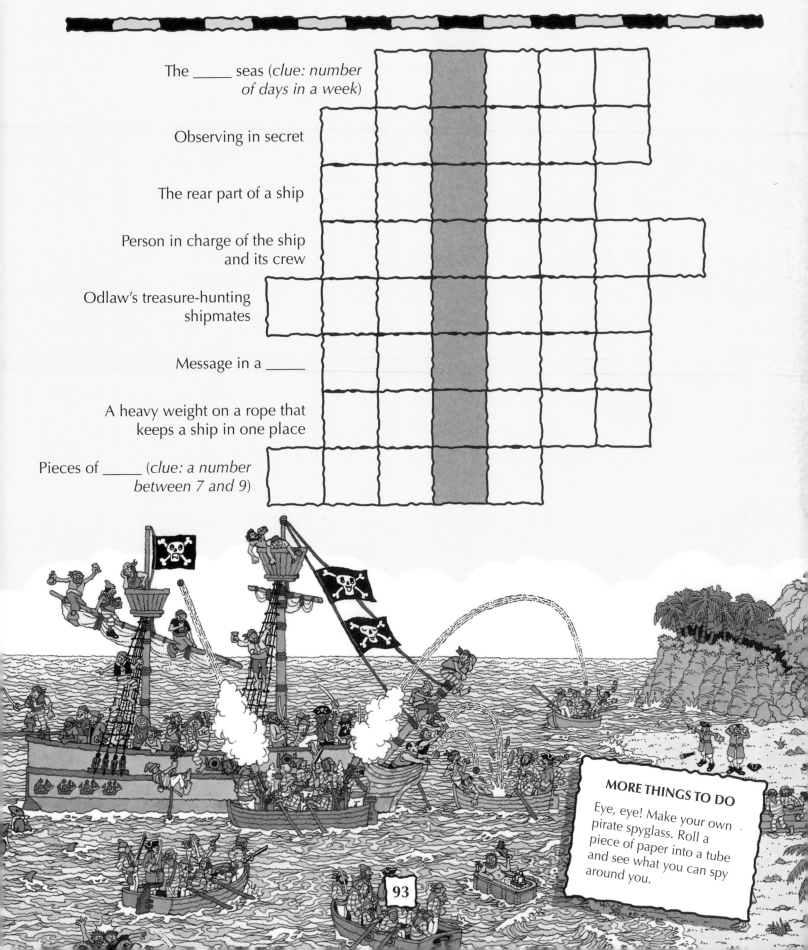

MORE THINGS TO DO

Eye, eye! Make your own pirate spyglass. Roll a piece of paper into a tube and see what you can spy around you.

93

WHAT A CATCH!

Odlaw's fishing for treasure.
Follow his line to find out what he caught.

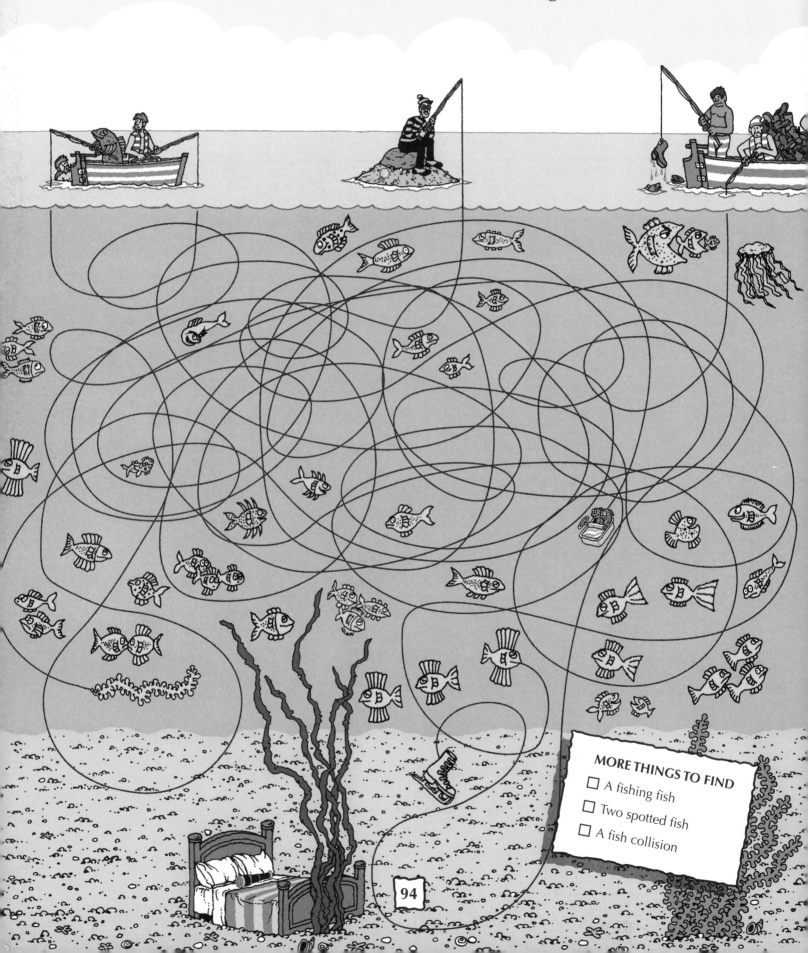

MORE THINGS TO FIND

☐ A fishing fish

☐ Two spotted fish

☐ A fish collision

94

SWAMPY SWIRL

Read Odlaw's swampy, swirly message by turning the page counter-clockwise. Beware: the message is written backward!

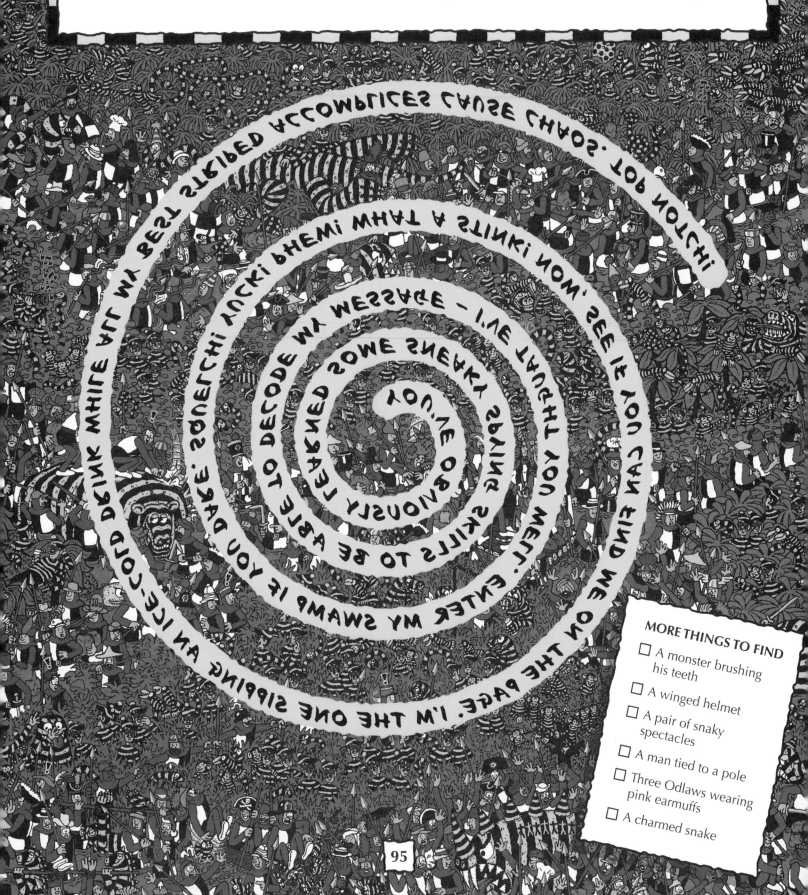

MORE THINGS TO FIND

- ☐ A monster brushing his teeth
- ☐ A winged helmet
- ☐ A pair of snaky spectacles
- ☐ A man tied to a pole
- ☐ Three Odlaws wearing pink earmuffs
- ☐ A charmed snake

BY MY CALCULATIONS, WE'RE NORTH OF NOWHERE UNLESS YOU'VE FOUND MY BINOCULARS. I'VE BARTERED WITH THE CAPTAIN FOR THIS CLUE, BUT I HOPE YOU KNOW HOW TO SPEAK PIRATE:

"AVAST! YE LANDLOCKED LUBBERS WILL BE SENT ON A BILGE-SUCKING SHANTY UNLESS YE HEAVE HO AND PILLAGE THE DARKEST TUNNELS TO UNCOVER ME MATEY'S BINOCULARS."

Odlaw

Can you spot where these pictures come from in Odlaw's chapter? Be careful: one is from somewhere else in the book!

ODLAW'S BINOCULARS CHECKLIST

Wait, there's more! Look back through the pictures and find . . .

- ☐ A boy dangling a spider from a stick
- ☐ An Odlaw wearing boots
- ☐ Two swordfish
- ☐ Four gray vultures
- ☐ A set of human-size weighing scales
- ☐ An angry musketeer
- ☐ Two yellow-and-black striped top hats
- ☐ A seabed
- ☐ Eight sharks waiting for their dinner
- ☐ A red monster
- ☐ A man in a bath boat

ONE LAST THING . . .

Remember those silhouettes on page 91 that you couldn't find? One appears in the other player's scene. The remaining two appear elsewhere in this book.

THAT WAS EPIC! WELL DONE!
THANKS FOR TRACKING DOWN OUR PRECIOUS THINGS—
WE'D BE LOST WITHOUT THEM. HA, HA!

ANSWERS TO SOME OF THE TRICKIEST
PUZZLES FOLLOW. DON'T GIVE UP ON THE
OTHERS—ASK YOUR FRIENDS TO HELP
IF YOU ARE STUCK.

AND THE ADVENTURE ISN'T OVER
QUITE YET! REMEMBER GATHERING
THE INGREDIENTS FOR WIZARD
WHITEBEARD'S SPELL? IT CREATED
SEVERAL RARE GOLDEN SEALS, THE
NUMBER OF WHICH IS REVEALED
ON PAGE 76. CAN YOU FIND
THEM BEFORE ODLAW'S
PIRATE FRIENDS DO?

HAPPY HUNTING!

Waldo

ANSWERS

★ WALDO'S KEY ★

p. 8 TRAVEL ESSENTIALS
MORE THINGS TO DO
rmcae epi = cream pie; dre eons = red nose;
niuylecc = unicycle

p. 10 RED-NOSE RUNAROUND
This is the shortest route.

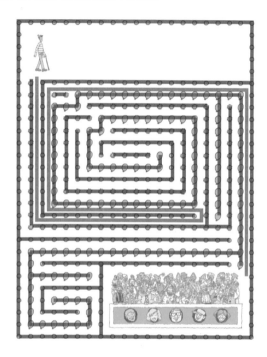

p. 14 PYRAMID PUZZLE

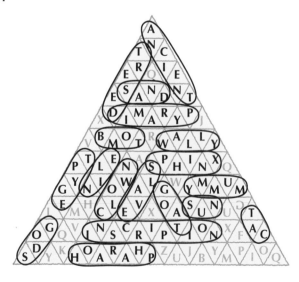

MORE THINGS TO FIND
There are 121 triangles in the puzzle.

p. 17 MOON-MAZE MAYHEM

p. 19 BALLOON BEDLAM

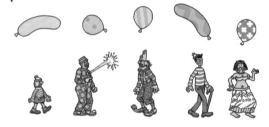

MORE THINGS TO DO
The missing pattern is the dotted balloon.

p. 20 WILD AND WACKY W'S

p. 21 SILLY STAMP SNAP

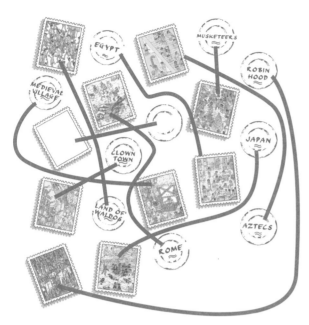

p. 24 WALDO'S KEY CHECKLIST

Page 13 has the most red noses.

★ WOOF'S BONE ★

p. 26 TO THE TAIL END

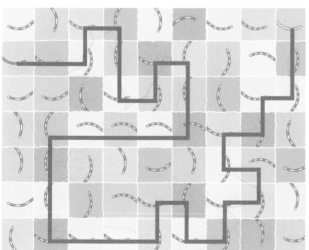

p. 28 WHO'S WHO?

OWOF	WOOF
GIMNCIAA	MAGICIAN
OADWL	WALDO
ALODW AWCTERH	WALDO WATCHER
VEMCANA	CAVEMAN
IPARET	PIRATE
RIOSNRAU	DINOSAUR
CTAROA	ACROBAT
IGHNKT	KNIGHT
GIKINV	VIKING

MORE THINGS TO DO
Write an anagram of your name in the empty box in the left-hand column.

p. 31 CONNECT THE BONES

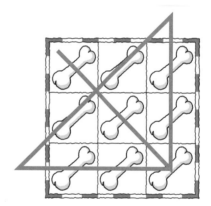

MORE THINGS TO DO

There are 14 squares in the grid.

p. 32 FLOWER POWER

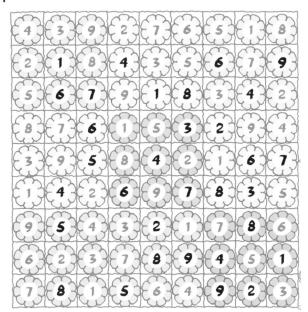

p. 33 BULL'S-EYE!

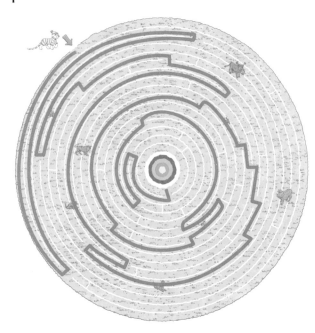

p. 34 WOOF'S WORD WHEEL

It's as hard as rock — stone; *Woof's favorite thing* — bone; *Used to sniff* — nose; *Heads, shoulders, knees, and ___* — toes; *Woof is one of these* — dog

p. 35 TRUTH OR TAILS?

1. True. 2. False. Answer: *p arasaurolophus*.
3. True. 4. True. 5. False. Answer: their diet — herbivores eat vegetation, and carnivores eat meat. 6. True: *tyrannosaurus rex*.
7. True. 8. False. Answer: it had two wings. 9. True. 10. True.

ONE MORE THING
Stegosaurus

p. 37 DIGGING FOR GOLD

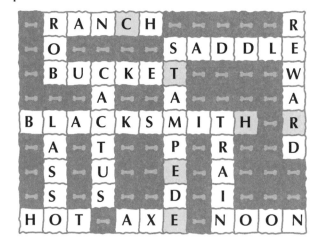

MORE THINGS TO DO
C / THREE

p. 38 NUMBER CRUNCHING

MORE THINGS TO DO
The circled cloud has the highest value.

p. 39 DOG'S DINNER

Ready, steady, go! The race is on! My canine friends and I are chasing our favorite food groups — sausages, bones, cats, and even mailmen!

MORE THINGS TO FIND
The word *wow* appears seven times.

p. 41 PLAY BALL

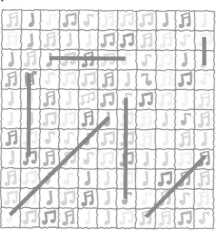

★ WENDA'S CAMERA ★

p. 47 BUSY BANDSTAND

Drum – sticks; clarinet – reed; conductor – baton; trombone – mouthpiece; violin – bow; triangle – rod; piano – keys

Wenda's favorite song is "Walking in a Winter Wonderland."

p. 48 A COLORFUL TUNE

p. 50 WOBBLY WORD LADDERS

p. 54 COSTUME COSTS

1 hat	$1
1 tie	$2
1 tie	$2
1 shirt	$3
1 shirt	$3
1 jacket	$4
$ =	15

p. 55 BOX BAMBOOZLE

MORE THINGS TO DO
The cube has seven other three-sided combinations (eight in total).

p. 56 OH, CRUMBS!

eggs; butter; flour; chocolate chips; sugar; cherries; cream

p. 59 DANCING SILHOUETTES

MORE THINGS TO FIND
Wenda's favorite dance is the waltz.

WIZARD WHITEBEARD'S ★ SCROLL ★

p. 62 STARS AND STRIPES

The path marked in yellow leads to Wizard Whitebeard's star.

MORE THINGS TO FIND
The path in blue crosses the most paths.

p. 63 SOMETHING FISHY

p. 64 SPELL-TACULAR!

Magic makes much mayhem.

p. 65 GIANT GAME

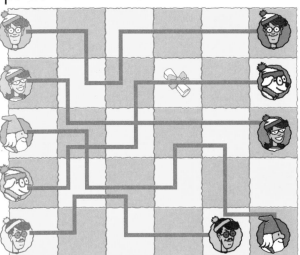

p. 66 MIX-UP MADNESS

p. 68 WORD CASTLE

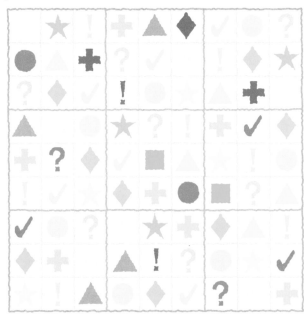

MORE THINGS TO FIND
The two magic words are "Open Sesame."

p. 70 GENIE-OUS!

p. 72 FRUIT PUNCH

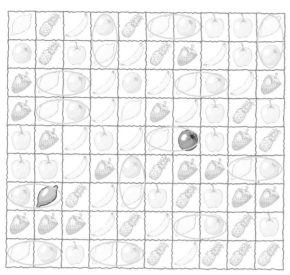

p. 75 WHICH WITCH IS WHICH?

1. Mystic Martha
2. Noisy Norma
3. Wicked Wartie
4. Tangle-Toes Tina
5. Moorb Hctiw

p. 76 MAGIC NUMBER

The magic number is 5.

★ ODLAW'S ★ BINOCULARS

p. 83 TOP FIENDS

Warty Gretel | Heave-Ho Henry | Captain Cutlass | Hungry Growler

MORE THINGS TO DO
Highest spying skills: Warty Gretel
Most courageous: Hungry Growler
Most terrifying: Heave-Ho Henry
Crystal Ball: Warty Gretel

p. 84 SKULDUGGERY

p. 86 SLIPPERY SEARCH

p. 88 SNAKING WORDS

A sea-traveling invader—Viking; *A sword-swishing soldier*—musketeer; *A skeletal symbol used by pirates*—skull and crossbones

p. 90 SNAKES AND LADDERS

Waldo wins the game!
His first move takes him to square 4
Second move: to square 10
Third move: to square 25 (up a ladder)
Fourth move: to square 13 (down a snake)
Fifth move: to square 28 (up a ladder)
Sixth move: to square 30

p. 92 LAND AHOY!

7 yellow birds; 5 pairs of sunglasses;
6 yellow fish; 7 yellow cream pies;
11 yellow balls; 5 black-and-yellow-striped
sleeves; 8 black mustaches = page 49

p. 93 PIRATEY PUZZLE

S	E	V	E	N		
S	P	Y	I	N	G	
S	T	E	R	N		
C	A	P	T	A	I	N
P	I	R	A	T	E	S
B	O	T	T	L	E	
A	N	C	H	O	R	
E	I	G	H	T		

p. 94 WHAT A CATCH!

p. 95 SWAMPY SWIRL

You've obviously learned some *sneaky* spying skills to be able to decode my message—I've taught you well. Enter my swamp if you dare. Squelch! Yuck! Phew! What a stink! Now, see if you can find me on the page. I'm the one sipping an ice-cold drink while all my best striped accomplices cause chaos. Top notch!

ONE LAST THING . . .

See if you can find Waldo, Woof (but only his tail), Wenda, Wizard Whitebeard, and Odlaw roaming outside their chapters!